FOR

LC  TLB

LITTLE TIGER PRESS

1 The Coda Centre, 189 Munster Road, London SW6 6AW

www.littletiger.co.uk

First published in Great Britain 2016

This edition published in Great Britain 2016

Text and illustrations copyright © Connah Brecon 2016

Connah Brecon has asserted his right to be identified as the author and illustrator
of this work under the Copyright, Designs and Patents Act, 1988

A CIP catalogue record for this book is available from the British Library

All rights reserved • ISBN 978-1-84869-274-9

Printed in China • LTP/1800/1444/0216

2 4 6 8 10 9 7 5 3 1

THIS LITTLE TIGER BOOK
BELONGS TO:

_____

_____

_____

PAWS McDRAW

~ THE FASTEST DOODLER IN THE WEST ~

CONNAH BRECON

LITTLE TIGER PRESS
London

Meet Paws McDraw.
The fastest doodler in the west!

So when the bunnies were in trouble who did they turn to? Paws McDraw!

At the well, Timmy was
in trouble. Deep trouble.

Paws pulled out his pencil
and started to sketch.

Then he pulled Timmy
up, up, up to safety!

"Hooray for Paws McDraw!"
cried the bunnies when Timmy
was high and dry.

They carried their hero
home to celebrate.

The bunnies threw a crazy cupcake carnival
in Paws' honour.

(Because y'all know bunnies
LOVE cupcakes, right?)

What an extravaganza of icing
and sprinkles it was! Everyone was
having a rootin'-tootin' time until . . .

. . . in burst
the Rascally Raccoon Gang.

Those lean, mean cupcake rustlers started terrorising the town!

Paws knew what had to be done.

Someone had to stop the raccoons.

And that someone was *him*.

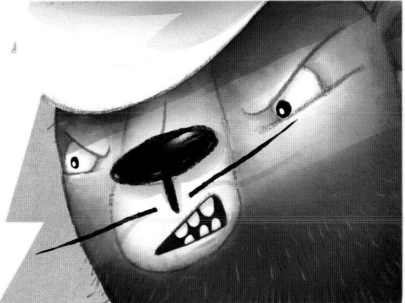

Paws was quick on the draw. He started to doodle . . .

and soon those raccoons were all tied up!

But in the blink of an eye,
they'd snipped their way free!
Paws needed a new plan. And fast.

. . . all locked up!

They were licked.

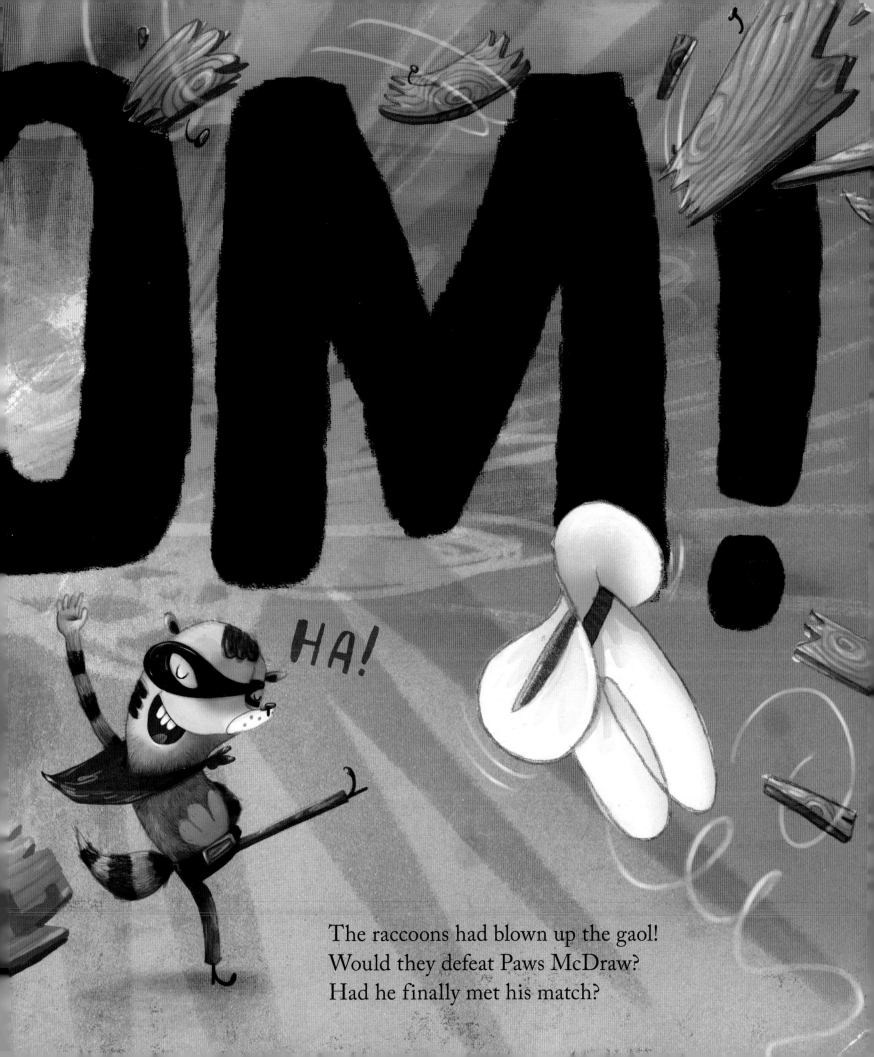

The raccoons had blown up the gaol!
Would they defeat Paws McDraw?
Had he finally met his match?

Paws was in real trouble! He was out of ideas! He needed a recipe for success!!

And, as the baker handed him his pencil, Paws had a brainwave.

With a fabulous moustache and top hat he turned the baker into a . . .

...MAGICIAN!

(Because y'all know bunnies LOVE magic, right?!)

HEY PESTO!
mix Lightly
FOCUS POGUS!
GAS mark 3
FABRACADABRA!
BUTTER-CREAM
AND
SPRINKLES
ON TOP!

With a swish of his wand and a few magic words the baker turned those terrible raccoons into . . .

"Woo hoo!" cried the bunnies as they chased the not-so-Rascally Raccoon cupcakes out of town.

Yup, Paws had saved the day again!
(With a bit of help from his friends.)

Three cheers for mighty
Paws McDraw!

FUEL THEIR IMAGINATIONS
WITH THESE WONDERFUL TALES
FROM LITTLE TIGER PRESS!

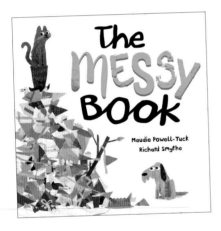

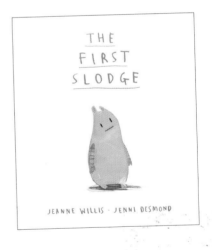

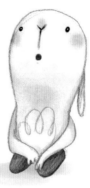

For information regarding any of the above titles or for our catalogue, please contact us:
Little Tiger Press, 1 The Coda Centre, 189 Munster Road, London SW6 6AW
Tel: 020 7385 6333 • E-mail: contact@littletiger.co.uk • www.littletiger.co.uk